Horace the Horrible

A Knight Meets His Match

by Jackie French Koller

illustrated by Jackie Urbanovic

Marshall Cavendish ~ New York

Cavendish Children's Books
Marshall Cavendish, 99 White Plains Road, Tarrytown, NY 10591
www.marshallcavendish.com

Library of Congress Cataloging-in-Publication Data
Koller, Jackie French.
Horace the Horrible : a knight meets his match / written by Jackie
French Koller ; illustrated by Jackie Urbanovic
p. cm.
Summary: The fearsome knight Horace tries to prove to his niece that he is as good as his brother, the
King, while all she really wants is someone to help her stop missing her father.
ISBN 0-7614-5150-1
[1. Knights and knighthood—Fiction. 2. Princesses—Fiction. 3.
Uncles—Fiction. 4. Sibling rivalry—Fiction.] I. Urbanovic, Jackie,
ill. II. Title.
PZ7.K833 Ho 2003
[E]—dc21
2002155921

The text of this book is set in Journal Ultra.
The illustrations are rendered in watercolor and pencil.

Book design by Virginia Pope
Printed in China

First edition
1 3 5 6 4 2

To Paul Joseph,
   the Adorable
         —J.F.K.

To Susan,
   who is a real-life
   Minuette: able to see
   what others cannot
   and brave enough
   to challenge giants
         —J.U.

Princess Minuette stared up at the name on the front door of her uncle's castle.

"Is my uncle really horrible?" she asked Friar Tim.

"His enemies certainly think so," said Friar Tim. He lifted the great doorknocker and let it fall.

A moment later the door flew open.

"I don't want any!" boomed Horace the Horrible.

"Please Sire," said Friar Tim. "I'm not selling anything. I am sent by your brother, the King."

"Hmmph," said Horace. "What does the Royal Big Wig want now?"

"He sent you this." Friar Tim stepped aside, and there stood Minuette.

"That!" roared Horace. "Why, that's a . . . child!"

"Precisely," said the friar. "It is your niece, Minuette. The King has the flu. He asks that you look after Minuette until he is well."

"That's impossible!" blustered Horace. "I've dragons to slay, armies to vanquish."

"Sorry," said Friar Tim. He gave Minuette a little push, said good-bye, and left.

"But. . . this
can't be!" shouted Horace.
Minuette stared at the high,
stone walls and leering gargoyles. It
was nothing like home. She sniffled.
Horace glared at her. Minuette began to sob.
"Great galloping gargoyles!" Horace bellowed.
"What's wrong?"
"I miss my daddy,"
said Minuette.

"Oh, Daddy faddy," said Horace. "I can do anything that swellhead can do. Come. Let's slay a dragon." He lifted Minuette up on his horse and rode off.

At last they heard a roar.

"Here's a dragon now!" shouted Sir Horace. "Down you go!" He lowered Minuette from the saddle. She grabbed his sword. "What are you doing?" he cried, his eyes on the approaching dragon. "Give that back. Hurry!"

Minuette picked up a stick and put it in Horace's hand.

Holding the stick high, Sir Horace charged.
Flames burst from the dragon's mouth and smoke
filled the air. There was a great deal of roaring
and shrieking, then a slightly scorched Sir Horace
charged back out of the smoke.

"THIS IS A STICK!" he shouted.

"I know," said Minuette.

"I could have been killed!" Sir Horace roared.

"So could the dragon," said Minuette, "and I still miss my daddy."

"Oh, Daddy raddy," Sir Horace blustered. "Your daddy couldn't fight a dragonfly. Come on, let's vanquish an army." He scooped up Minuette and galloped off again. Over hill and dale they rode until they came upon a vast army.

"Ah, here we go," said Sir Horace. He lowered Minuette to the ground and raced down into the valley.

Minuette heard clashing swords and
thundering hooves. She saw the great army
flee into the hills. Sir Horace rode back with
a flagstaff in his hand.

"For you, my lady," he said.

Minuette unfurled the flag and looked at it.

"Uncle," she said. "This is our flag. You just
vanquished our army!"

Sir Horace lifted his visor and squinted.
"Oh drat!" he mumbled.

"I miss my daddy." Minuette sniffed.

"Daddy shmaddy," said Horace. "Your daddy couldn't vanquish an army of ants! Let's go find some damsels in distress."

East and west and north and south they
rode—to the farthest corners of the kingdom,
but there were no damsels to be found.
Discouraged, Sir Horace sat down beneath a
tree for some lunch and a short nap.

While Horace snored, Minuette gazed at a
tall, stone tower in the distance. Away from
her uncle she crept, across the meadow she
ran, and up the tower stairs she climbed.

"Help! Help!" Minuette cried.

Sir Horace sprang to his feet. "A damsel!" he cried. "Fear not, my lady! Help is on the way!" He leapt to his horse, charged across the meadow, scaled the tower walls, and hurled himself through the window.

"You could have taken the stairs," said Minuette.

Sir Horace stared. "You!" he cried. "I thought I heard a damsel in distress."

"Uncle," said Minuette. "I AM a damsel in distress."

Horace looked doubtful. "How so?" he asked.

"I miss my daddy!" shouted Minuette.

"Oh, Daddy waddy!" shouted Sir Horace. He grabbed Minuette's hand and dragged her back out to the meadow.

"Just tell me one thing your daddy does better than I do," he demanded.

"He hugs," said Minuette.

"He . . . **what**?" Sir Horace choked.

"He hugs," said Minuette. "That's all I want. Not a dragon, not an army, not a damsel in distress. Just a hug."

"Pfff," said Horace. "We can't have that. I'm far too hard and prickly for hugging."

"You could take your armor off,"
said Minuette.

"Take my . . . ! Are you mad? I haven't had
my armor off in public since I was a knave."

"But my daddy—" Minuette began.

Horace rolled his eyes.
"Oh, all right!" he barked.
He took off his helmet, his
breastplate, his mail suit,
and his gloves. He squinted
in the sun. "I don't think
I like this," he said.

"Sit down," said Minuette.
Sir Horace sat.

Minuette crawled into his lap. "Now, hug."

Very carefully, Horace put his arms around her.

Minuette snuggled against his chest. "Thank you, Uncle Horace," she said.

Sir Horace blushed. "No one will ever call me Horace the Horrible again."

"Is that so bad?" asked Minuette.

Sir Horace considered. Without his armor on, he could hear the birds singing and smell the meadow flowers. He could feel the sun on his shoulders and the cool breeze in his hair. He hugged Minuette tighter.

"Maybe not," he said.